WINTER ROSE IN DARKNESS

MEYARI MCFARLAND

CONTENTS

Special Offer	v
Other Books by Meyari McFarland:	vii
Winter Rose in Darkness	1
Author's Note: Ten Days of Harmony	10
1. Hemlock	11
2. Maple	21
Other Books by Meyari McFarland:	31
Afterword	33
Author Bio	35

SPECIAL OFFER

The rainbow has infinite shades, just as this collection covers the spectrum of fictional possibilities.

From contemporary romances like *The Shores of Twilight Bay* to dark fantasy like *A Lone Red Tree* and out to SF futures in *Child of Spring*, *Iridescent* covers the gamut of time, space and genre.

Meyari McFarland shows her mastery in this first omnibus collection of her short fiction. Twenty-five amazing stories, all with queer characters going on adventures, solving mysteries, and falling in love are here in the first Rainbow Collection.

And now you can get this massive collection of short queer fiction, all of it with the happy endings you love, *for free!*

Sign up here for your free copy of Iridescent now!

OTHER BOOKS BY MEYARI MCFARLAND:

Day Hunt on the Final Oblivion

Day of Joy

Immortal Sky

A New Path

Following the Trail

Crafting Home

Finding a Way

Go Between

Like Arrows of Fate

Out of Disaster

The Shores of Twilight Bay

Coming Together

Following the Beacon

The Solace of Her Clan

You can find these and many other books at www.MDR-Publishing.com. We are a small independent publisher focusing on LGBT content. Please sign up for our mailing list to get regular updates on the latest preorders and new releases and a free ebook!

Copyright ©2024 by Mary Raichle

Print ISBN: 978-1-64309-128-0

Cover image

Deposit Photo ID# 211687646 by luminastock

All rights reserved. No part of this publication may be reproduced or transmitted in any form or by any means, electronic or mechanical, including photocopy, recording or any information storage and retrieval system, without permission in writing from the publisher.

Requests for permission to make copies of any part of the work should be emailed to publisher@mdr-publishing.com.

This book is also available in TPB format from all major retailers.

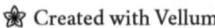 Created with Vellum

This story is dedicated to my Mom, gone but never forgotten.

WINTER ROSE IN DARKNESS

Kaitlyn wrapped her favorite fleece blanket around her shoulders, rubbing her cheek against its floof. She'd never had anything fleece that was this soft, this warm, this much like being wrapped in a cloud of winter warmth. The fabric was soft cream with fuzzy grey roses that looked like she was seeing a rose garden through thick fog.

It felt like fog, like the softest kitten belly fluff, like the pure warmth of snuggling up next to her mother when she was very small and cuddling under whichever afghan her mother had been making at the time. Except without all the complaints, bitching about Kaitlyn's faithless father, and questions about Kaitlyn's schoolwork.

No, she wasn't going to let her mother colonize her mind tonight. Kaitlyn had spent enough years coping with her mother's behavior. She didn't know how many nights had been fractured by running on the hamster wheel in her head as she had arguments in her head with her mother, and then given herself nightmares of still being six with her mother looming over her.

So no. No thinking about Mother.

The house was still around Kaitlyn. Not silent. No house as old as theirs could be dead-quiet. There were creaks and pops from the house slowly settling down on its foundation like an old cat lowering itself down on its favorite cushion for a nap. Wind blew outside, not hard. Just enough to whistle through the eaves outside the bedroom window. It smelled like rain, damp and green with the last lawn mowing of the season.

Three in the morning was always a quiet time.

Kaitlyn didn't intend to get up at three. It just happened. Every night.

She had been dreaming about work, fingers tapping away at her new mechanical keyboard that was so quiet and soft and easy to use. Whenever she had glanced down at the keyboard in the dream, it shimmered between teal and forest green, perfectly soothing and lovely. Kaitlyn smiled.

She'd known, quite clearly, that she was typing up a report for her boss so that she could present it to top management next week. The keyboard worked perfectly even though Kaitlyn couldn't read the letters on the keys. Whenever she typed, hieroglyphics showed up on the screen, Unicode nonsense mixed with Ancient Egyptian and odd little squiggles that a toddler might make.

Music played from nowhere, a strange mix of songs Kaitlyn had stored on her phone and music that didn't exist except in her dreams. The music had switched from upbeat and bright, to ominous as Kaitlyn looked at her computer screen, suspended between two long vines of purple-green ivy, and tried to sort out whether or not she'd made a typo. The not-letters on the screen had twisted and waved at her.

Kaitlyn had blinked.

The music stopped mid-beat.

And she was awake, eyes blurry as she looked across the

bedroom towards her little walk-in closet and the door to her bathroom. At three, the bathroom looked like a window to a far-away lighthouse, blinking rhythmically as her toothbrush charged. The walk-in closet was a cave, dark and dim with only hints of stalactites in the place of sleeves, dresses and Kaitlyn's rarely-worn jeans.

Jesse hadn't moved a muscle, snoring away as Kaitlyn eased from the bed and claimed her favorite fleece blanket from the foot of the bed. No reason to wake him when she was the one who couldn't sleep through the night.

She'd been that way since she was a baby, never quite overcoming the desire to be up and moving in the dark hours of the night. Mother used to lock Kaitlyn in her bedroom just to keep her from wandering and breaking something.

No. No Mother.

Especially no memories of her old bedroom with the lock on the outside so that Kaitlyn couldn't escape.

The house creaked as Kaitlyn quietly shuffled through the hallways. It was old, not historical register old, but old enough that the wiring was quirky, the plumbing needed to be torn out entirely and replaced someday in the not too distant future, and the roof had had to be torn off and completely redone a year and a half ago.

That'd been an ouch. Kaitlyn smiled, tugging her fleece blanket up to her chin and hugging herself with it. So much money, way more than any of them had wanted, but they'd pooled their savings, considered their options, and gone for the top of the line roof that had a transferrable 50-year warrantee. No more leaks and no more worries about the house rotting from the top down.

Light leaked out under the bedroom door on the other side of the hall.

Anders had fallen asleep reading again. When Kaitlyn

peeked into his room, Anders had a Kindle on his face, a textbook on his belly and an iridescent purple fountain pen, capped thank goodness, loosely clasped in his hand.

She shook her head, rescued him from the reading, and covered him up with his version of her favorite fleece blanket. Anders' fleece was red and green plaid with white stripes. It was very Christmas-y and a double-thickness, so she wasn't too surprised that he'd kicked it off for studying.

He smiled and sighed and rolled onto his belly once she covered him up. One foot kicked out from under the blanket, ensuring that he wouldn't overhead. She wasn't sure how the monsters under the bed didn't grab him. Anders' cats were known ankle-grabbers.

Kaitlyn slipped out of Anders' bedroom, leaving the door cracked open for when the monsters under the bed decided it was time for their four-thirty scamper though the hallways. A huge jaw-cracking yawn didn't stop her amble through the house. Anders needed his sleep. He was so close to his Masters. She couldn't remember the last time he'd slept just because he wanted to, not because he'd fallen face-down in his books.

Tomorrow, Kaitlyn would get Rian and Lin to help her make Anders' favorite 7-Up cake. He needed a break and making that cake would be the perfect lure to get him away from his books and studying. She tapped her bottom lip thoughtfully with a blanket-wrapped fingertip and then headed downstairs to the first floor.

Rian and Lin's bedroom light was on.

Kaitlyn tiptoed to their door, gently pushing it open.

They'd spent so much time making their shared bedroom perfect for the two of them. Every single inch of the walls was covered with art. Between the two of them, Rian had claimed that they had more than a thousand pieces of original art, all bought at various conventions, farmer's markets and craft fairs they'd gone to.

Personally, Kaitlyn liked Lin's paintings best. They hadn't put one up in their bedroom, Lin protesting that she couldn't possibly put one of her crap pieces up when they had so much good art. Kaitlyn had deliberately glared right in Lin's eyes at the next craft fair as she pointed at a gorgeous painting of a world tree with rainbow leaves that looked like stained glass.

Lin had blushed as she wrapped it for Kaitlyn to take home. She'd blushed as Jesse helped Kaitlyn hang it in her bedroom. She blushed even now when she came to gather laundry when it was Lin's turn to wash clothes.

It was gorgeous.

So very beautiful. Kaitlyn shook her head at the two girls curled up together on their bed. Their fleece blanket was purple with rainbow-maned unicorns prancing across it. Jesse had flinched when Rian picked it, turning speaking, traumatized eyes to Kaitlyn.

She'd grinned and bought the fleece with delight.

It had taken more than a little bit of work to find the right rainbow-striped bias tape for the edging, but it had been worth it to watch Rian and Lin giggle as they cuddled together under their blanket. Even Jesse had smiled at their delight, mustache bristling and then twitching as Jesse pressed his lips together so that he wouldn't openly grin at the girls being so adorable.

Kaitlyn turned their lights down so that the room wasn't as bright. They'd sleep better if they didn't have the overhead lights blazing down through their eyelids. The rest of the lights in the room, all programmed to go through rainbow colors in soothing cascades, were more than bright enough to keep Rian from a panic attack if she woke in the middle of the night like Kaitlyn always did.

Yes, there would have to be a 7-Up cake tomorrow. Every time they made a cake, Anders drew away from his book to poke in the cabinets for the antique Bundt cake pan he'd gotten from an estate sale. It reminded him of his grandmother, who was an absolute battleax, but despite her caustic tongue and combative personality, she could bake.

She could *bake*, Anders always said. His eyes got wide as he dusted off the facets of the Bundt pan with a soft rag prior to carrying it to the sink for a good wash. A steak cooked by Gramma Smith was as good as eating shoe leather, but the dinner roll that came with it would be soft and flakey, rich while still being light. The dessert that came after dinner, every dinner, made up for the inedible entrée.

Cakes with cloud-centers so light you'd think they were air. Chocolate cakes dense and rich and fudgy, as thick as a brownie but with hints of cinnamon and almond. Pies that could be their own meal.

Kaitlyn chuckled softly as she checked that they had the cup and a half of butter they needed. Plenty of that, yes. The lemons in the crisper drawer were still heavy for their size. They'd be plenty juicy for flavoring the cake and the thin frosting Anders loved to beat while the cake cooled. Lots of flour, too. Good thing she'd managed to get a bag when she got to the grocery store last.

The fridge shut with a dull thud that shouldn't wake the girls. Kaitlyn would claim that there was no way that it would wake anyone in the house, but Jesse had always had ears like a bat. The man swore up and down that he could hear garage door openers which was just ridiculous. Kaitlyn shook her head as she drifted out of the kitchen, blanket tugged tight around her hips.

Outside, rain began to fall finally.

At first, it was a quiet patter against the plastic awning panels on the back porch's overhang. Jesse had spent hours this last summer securing the panels so that they wouldn't rattle or bang when the wind blew. The previous owners had barely secured the panels so for the first few years they'd lived in the house, every single wind storm brought thumps, bangs and screeches from the plastic panels trying to escape the overhang.

Kaitlyn had always known a storm was coming in by the sound of the wind humming over the panels. Now they drummed in the rain, steady as bedrock instead of flying like curtains. She leaned against the French doors that opened onto the back yard, smiling at the sound of the rain drumming down.

It was like the music she'd dreamed; random, unpredictable, unearthly beautiful. Nothing human lived in the sound of the rain making music on the overhang. Kaitlyn shut her eyes, shivering despite her wonderful rose garden blanket. The back-door's weather stripping so needed to be replaced. A breeze zipped over her toes, chilling them. Another skittered over the crown of her head, forcing its way in through the failing seals on the French doors.

Another project they would need to save for. More money to scrounge up somehow. Kaitlyn shook her head as she turned away from the back door and went to the door into the garage. It was properly and securely locked. Good. No chance of Mother sneaking inside and haranguing Kaitlyn, not that she was even in this state.

She opened it and peeked inside out of pure habit. No one could blame her for making sure, after all. Well, no one that Kaitlyn loved and considered a real family would care. They all made a point of locking the doors at night and telling Kaitlyn that they'd checked them all. No windows unlocked on the ground floor, no trees near the walls so that someone, Mother, could climb up and get in.

Kaitlyn's heart beat faster as she slowly opened the door

to the garage, hard-earned instinct telling her to be wary even as the rational day-time part of her mind scoffed and told her not to be so silly.

In the darkness of the night, with only a few lights from Rian's workbench on the other side of the garage, the cars looked like slumbering oxen. Big dark lumps that didn't move at all. The shelves full of carefully labeled boxes full of Legos and board games hadn't moved at all. Rian's tools were on their hooks on the pegboard. Even the shop vac had been tucked into its corner under the workbench, exactly where it was supposed to be.

Kaitlyn smiled and leaned against the door, just taking the garage in. Really, they'd done such a nice job organizing it. All the shovels and brooms, rakes and hedge trimmers, hung from hooks on the walls. The step ladder Jesse preferred for working on the overhang and trimming their dwarf apple and plum trees hung up near the ceiling, just as it was supposed to.

She nodded and locked the door to the garage. Checked the French doors and nodded that it was locked and deadbolted just as it should be. One by one, Kaitlyn made a slow, quiet circuit of the windows and doors on the first floor.

Not one thing was out of place. Nothing was unlocked. The rain hammered down outside, beating against the walls and the overhang like fairy drummers intent on leading an army into battle. They must be getting ready to go fight against the wind fairies who'd dragged them here before the rainstorm started. They would fight in the darkness of the night, waging battle with each other until the dawn came and chased them all back into the darkest shadows.

Kaitlyn laughed silently at herself before slowly climbing the stairs back up to the second floor. Really, if she was making up stories about rain and wind fairies, she needed to go back to bed.

Maybe she'd dream about it once she put her head back down on the pillow. That would be lovely.

She got a quick, quiet drink of water in the bathroom. Draped her wonderful rose garden blanket over the foot of the bed, just on her side. Jesse's side had almost no blankets. The man was such a furnace when he slept. It was amazing. Kaitlyn got colder, not hotter, when she slept.

He stirred as she slipped carefully back under the covers, surprised and not surprised that his hand was resting right where her shoulder would have been if she hadn't gotten up and gone wandering about the house.

"Everything safe?" Jesse rumbled, voice sleep-rough and unconcerned. If he opened his eyes, Kaitlyn couldn't see it in the darkness of their bedroom.

"Mhm," Kaitlyn murmured, kissing his knuckles. "Go back to sleep, love."

He smiled, mustache curling just enough that Kaitlyn could see it. Then he patted her shoulder, rubbed his face against his pillow and sighed as he dropped back asleep. His hand stayed on Kaitlyn's shoulder, warm and solid and comforting.

Kaitlyn curled up into a ball on her side of the bed, stretched one leg out and then put her hand over Jesse's.

She dropped off again easily as drums and flutes played wild, inhuman music in her dreams.

AUTHOR'S NOTE: TEN DAYS OF HARMONY

Sometimes you just want a quiet, calm, gentle story. Winter Rose was one of those stories for me. Kaitlyn's insomnia and midnight ramble through the house isn't too far from what my mom used to do and what I do from time to time.

Another story that has that gentle feel to it is Ten Days of Harmony which was previously published in the Happiness in Numbers anthology. It's a lovely novella, sweet and kind, so I really wanted to share a teaser of it with you here.

Hope you enjoy the sample!

1. HEMLOCK

*G*iang Nunes sat in xyr car, staring at the pack's home and wanting to fuss with xyr appearance. Somewhat. There was no way to change xyr mix of human and dryad features before meeting with the werewolves. The dryad side of xyr heritage showed clearly in the shifting colors of xyr hair, eyes and skin while the human side showed in xyr features, fingers, hands and limbs, all of which were as human as human could be.

Xyr boss had always said that they should present themselves as attractively as possible when meeting with the public. But Giang struggled with that. Xyr hair was growing into spring greens after the white of winter. At least xyr eyes had made the switch fully. Instead of the spooky ice-blue that always startled xem during January and February, xyr eyes were the green-gold of new aspen leaves with sunshine through them, bright and happy and... nervous.

Very nervous. Xyr powers always made things so difficult. Giang couldn't risk affecting others by deliberately projecting an aura; both professionally and personally that was inappropriate. Xyr family had told xem so many times that xe was influencing everyone around xem, even when Giang was certain xe wasn't.

Giang couldn't take the risk. So xe would have to face the pack's house with nothing more than xyr snub nose, motley hair and the proposal xe had been sent out to work on. And xe certainly wasn't going to portray xemself as either male or female given that dryads had no determinate gender whatsoever.

It was huge, one of the big old Victorian houses that'd survived the Opening. Mostly. Xe could see that the entire back half of the house had been replaced with more modern building materials but the front half maintained the old clapboard and graceful trim. Big tower with a bunch of windows and a porch that looked like it was halfway through being torn out and rebuilt.

The pack house sat at the very end of the cul-de-sac. While the old Victorian had survived the fire, transformation and death of the Opening, the other houses on the cul-de-sac clearly hadn't. To the left were two rebuilt ramblers. The first had been built with sculpted stone. The second with cob and straw bale, topped with a living roof that had sprouted vivid yellow flowers that were starting to fade. On the right were three Baba Yaga Huts, quietly scratching at the ground as they huddled together in the clearing they'd created since moving there.

A quiet neighborhood. Giang almost wished xe could live here but there was no way for xem to do that, not with the werewolf pack controlling the majority of the open land in this area. Xe didn't earn enough to afford even a tiny parcel of land and there was no way xe'd ever live in a Baba Yaga hut. Xe certainly couldn't wait long enough for one of their eggs to hatch and grow big enough for habitation, even if that was the best way to get a Baba Yaga hut that got along well with you.

Giang's boss had warned xem ahead of time that the werewolves controlled the hundred acres of land that sat right behind that house. It was fenced, owned and patrolled; the sort of place that you couldn't just walk in and start hunting on. Not even when all you were looking for was hard-to-find plants.

Gorgeous, too, full of big old pine trees mixed with broadleaf maple and mature cottonwood reaching up for the sky. Xe could see some poplar trees near the fence and a couple of surprising hemlock trees on the front yard. Those looked utterly unhealthy, which was no surprise. That much sunshine for a young seedling that usually grows under the canopy of thick cedar bows had to be half killing the poor things. They probably wouldn't survive out there long term unless the pack grew some shrubs around them.

Xe might just suggest it while xe was here. No reason for the poor seedlings to suffer when Giang could make a difference. Of course, Giang was the one sent here today because xe was the sort to care about the random seedlings, bits of moss and sword ferns that had to fill the pack's property. And without the pack's permission, there was no way that they would get what they needed for the Harmony.

Xe wasn't at all sure that xe was ready to meet an entire pack of werewolves by xemself. The sheer number of children inside was sure to be overwhelming and who knew if the alpha, Deidre MacClellen, would even have time to talk to Giang. Alphas were always so busy with the kids.

But sitting in xyr car wasn't going to get xem any closer to having permission to tromp through the pack's woods. Giang got out and gathered the promotional materials for the Harmony. Xe should've brought the little gift bag that xyr boss had pushed at xem but Giang thought that was so tacky. And poorly made. Giang couldn't give something that cheap to an Alpha. Xe'd just have to juggle brochures.

Or shove them in xyr back pocket. That worked, too.

Xe slowed as xe approached the front steps. Or what would have been front steps. The elaborately carved posts that supported the front overhang were still there but the porch itself had been torn out. Bits of rotted wood that had once been steps coated the soil underneath, mixed with huge amounts of pixie dust and webbing from a variety of spiders.

"They let pixies live under their deck?" Giang murmured as xe peered into the hole where the stairs should have been. "Well, that wasn't wise. I hope the foundation wasn't damaged."

"Nah, not damaged at all. The porch was totaled but they didn't get at the concrete. Actually, they were pretty careful to dig their burrows away from the foundation so yeah, house is fine."

Giang jumped and whirled, staring up and up at the very tall, very beautiful woman who stood grinning down at xem. At six foot at least, maybe more, Deidre MacClellan had sandy brown hair, a nose that had been broken and set poorly at some point and a gap between her front teeth that whistled as she laughed quietly at Giang's expense.

Deidre also had a dragon runt on her right arm, a canvas bag full of groceries in her other hand and a pair of werewolf pups sitting at her feet. They looked to be the age where four legs were faster and easier than two, leading to more time in pup form than might be common later in life. The pups both stared at Giang, tails wagging in that slow, speculative way that automatically made Giang's heart-rate pick up.

"Ah, Deidre MacClellan?" Giang asked because what else could xe say?

"That's me," Deidre said. Her nose wrinkled as she grinned at xem. "You from the city government? They left some half-assed message about requiring access to the pack lands for something."

"Yes, that's me," Giang said with a little sigh of annoyance. "Though I'd hoped that they would give you more information than that. We're not requiring anything. It's... well. Um. Perhaps we could discuss it inside?"

Xe fumbled for a business card and then shook xyr head. Deidre didn't have any hands free. How was she going to take it? Giang pulled the card and then offered xyr arms for the dragon runt who sniffed at xem and looked up to Deidre. She sniffed too and then nodded approval as she gave the dragon runt to Giang and took xyr card.

Giang grunted at the weight of the runt. Not so small anymore. His—because yes, this was a male dragon—his horns were just starting to poke through above his temples. At least the runt was growing well, though Giang had no idea what to do as his tail wrapped around xyr waist and he stared at her, ears cycling as he listened to xyr heart, Deidre, the pups and who knew what else?

"Pleased to meet you?"

"Nice!" the runt exclaimed before wrapping his arms around xyr shoulders and putting his head on xyr shoulder. His voice reverberated through Giang, his meaning carried as much by his innate draconic magic as by the sounds he made with his mouth. Dragon tongues were among the most mobile in the world so they didn't have to use too much magic to be heard.

"That's Mori," Deidre said with an approving nod. "Twins here are Mimi and Cece. Roger's getting more groceries with my oldest, Janie. My husband, Tyson, should be inside making dinner. We're using the back door until the porch is fixed."

"Ah, well, lead on?" Giang suggested. "What in the world happened with the porch?"

"Pixies," Deidre said as she led the way to the fence alongside the house. She'd tucked the card into the bag of groceries so she could open the door easily. "Let them live under the porch on the agreement that they'd protect us from vermin and not impact the foundations at all. Turns out that they eat the wood so yeah, porch fell apart."

"I went boom," Mori said, huffing a plume of steam through his nostrils. Not yet flaming. That was reassuring at least. Xyr hair wouldn't be burned off.

"And they bit him, so we've recently relocated them to the back yard," Deidre said, pointing towards a very nice, new pixie nest made of a huge pile of logs. The pixies whirled around it, humming in their multipart symphony of voices. "You know they can't breed if they don't have new nests? I can't believe that people deny pixies the right to have offspring. It's ridiculous!"

"Yes," Giang said. Xe stared up at Deidre, amazed that she was so offended over that. "It's… well, most people don't want pixies around at all. They are rather messy. And rather destructive."

Deidre grumbled something under her breath that xe couldn't understand. Probably something uncomplimentary. She was an Alpha, so Giang didn't question it. But if Deidre was this impressive, and beautiful, she must have a truly imposing mate. Most Alpha males were… fierce. Terrifyingly fierce as far as Giang was concerned. All teeth and claws and dominance rituals that Giang had never, ever been able to perform properly. Xe had too much dryad blood for that. Dryads simply didn't understand dominance in the right ways for Alpha males.

Deidre's scowl was so intimidating that Giang's stomach did flips as they climbed the back stairs, cubs scrambling up the stairs and yapping excitedly around their legs as they ran inside the instant the door was open. Xyr mother scowled like that every time Giang came home. Not that xe wanted to remember that right now. Xe had work to do. Crying xyr heart out and begging for forgiveness wasn't appropriate at all.

"Tyson, we got that guest from the city government," Deidre called as she kicked her shoes off.

"Yeah?" Tyson called back.

He sounded... mild. Giang blinked and then outright stared as Tyson came in to take the groceries. Where Deidre was tall and powerful, Tyson was short; barely half a head taller than Giang. Balding, fire-red hair and a kind smile that calmed Giang so quickly that it took xem a moment to realize there was magic behind it.

"You're a fire mage," Giang said and then blushed.

"Yep," Deidre said with a huge grin as Tyson blushed as red as his hair. "Nicest thing in the world to cuddle up against at night, you know?"

"I suppose so," Giang said. Xe looked at Mori who blinked back and then squirmed to be let down. Finally. "I've not dated much. People tend to... make assumptions about me because I have dryad blood."

That got scowls from both Deidre and Tyson so hopefully Giang wouldn't have to deal with any inept and highly annoying attempts from them trying to hit on xem. Xe stepped aside as a young man with an enveloping hoodie printed with the Fly High Angels logo came in carrying two bags of groceries. That must be Roger. He nodded to Giang, kicked off his shoes and then headed into the kitchen. The teenage girl that followed was clearly Deidre's child, big and strong. She was also clearly Tyson's daughter because she radiated that same warmth he did. So that would be Janie, the last member of the pack Deidre had named.

"We got the groceries," Janie said to her parents. "Go ahead and see what's up with the government rep. Though it better not be getting rid of either the pixies or the fairy dragon on the back forty. They're pack now and none of us are gonna care what the city government says about that."

"... You have a fairy dragon?" Giang asked, staring up at Janie. "Goodness, what kind? They're so rare in this area."

Janie blinked and then grinned as if Giang had passed a test of some sort. "Water. She's a cute little thing. We built a bridge over the entrance to her lair, so she'd be safe but I'm sure you'll meet her if you head out that way. She likes meeting people."

Janie marched off into the kitchen, leaving Giang with the twin urges to follow her to ask more questions or to run straight out into the forest so that she could meet the fairy dragon. A real fairy dragon, so close. Goodness, that was... so tempting.

"Come on," Deidre said. "Let's go out on the back porch. You look like you'd rather be outside anyway."

"You do have lovely trees," Giang said. Xe waited impatiently for Deidre and Tyson to pull their shoes back on. "Though I'm terribly worried about the hemlocks on the front lawn. They need much more shade than they're getting."

"Really?" Tyson asked. "The kids picked them to plant there because they were pretty and had soft needles."

"Oh, they do," Giang said, more than happy to talk about trees. "But they usually grow up in the shade of cedar trees. Some nice, quick-growing lilac would help them. Or spells to give them a bit more shade during the heat of the sun."

The back yard was a marvel of kids' toys, comfortable fire pit seating and barely growing grass. Too many feet trampling the grass. And paws. There were quite a few spots where the cubs had been digging; little holes scrabbled out of the dirt for playtime.

Tyson tossed a well-seasoned log of cedar into the firepit. It lit before it hit the ground, snapping and sparking cheerily.

"Not gonna bother you?" Deidre asked.

"Hmm?" Giang asked, and then started when xe realized that both Deidre and Tyson were staring at xem. "Oh, no. I don't mind fires like this at all. I've enough magic that I could put out a house fire if I wanted to. Thankfully I haven't had to. This is lovely. And not at all why I'm here. I'm so sorry. I shouldn't waste your time."

The logs were old, old enough that Giang felt no sense of the life they used to live. They were just food for the forest now, mulch in the making. It was such a comforting feeling that xe sighed and enjoyed it a moment before pulling out the brochures.

"We're working on the spells for the Harmony for the High Elves in Belleview," Giang explained. "And my department has been tasked with gathering the spell components. Sadly, a great many of them are terribly hard to find. The least bit of iron ruins some. And there are so few areas where we have untrammeled natural forest to gather the rest. My boss is working on the iron sensitive ones. He's got messages out all across the continent and is traveling a ridiculous amount at the moment."

"And so you came to us for our forest," Deidre said, sitting up and frowning at the threat of intrusion.

"Yes," Giang said. "I'd be personally gathering the plants because of my dryad blood. I can go and not harm the forest at all. Frankly, I'm quite hopeful that I'll find everything I need here. You have pixies tending to the woods and your pack and a baby dragon and goodness, a fairy dragon, too. I can't believe that. My boss will be so happy. He thought he'd have to travel down to the Amazon to find a fairy dragon."

"What do you need from us?" Tyson asked, interrupting xyr glee and excitement.

"Um, access?" Giang said, a little nervous about the way the two of them stared at xem. "To bring a bucket and trowel and, oh, some clippers. I anticipate it will take a good three months to gather everything. If it's all here. Some of it has to be harvested at particular times of the year. We've started months and months in advance so that we'd be sure to get everything in time."

"So it's not a one-time thing," Tyson said more cheerfully.

"Um, no?" Giang said. She turned to Deidre, who was laughing quietly and shaking her head at Tyson for some reason. "I'd probably need to visit at least once a week for the next few months. If that's all right."

"It's fine," Deidre said. "Come on. Let's take a quick tour so you know the lay of the land. All I ask is that you call ahead and then have one of us—one of the two of us, not the kids—escort you."

Giang beamed as xe jumped to xyr feet. "I can do that! Thank you so much!"

Really, that was far easier than xe'd expected. Giang couldn't wait to tell xyr boss.

Well. Xe could wait. Until after xe'd gotten xyr tour and heard all about the land from Deidre and Tyson.

2. MAPLE

Tyson leaned against the big maple closest to the creek as Rudenth the Adorable, their resident fairy dragon, shook water droplets from her delicate little wings. The last few weeks had been very interesting as he and Deidre escorted Giang around the property, making sure she had everything she needed for the Harmony.

Somehow, though, they'd not gotten out to Rudenth's stream before now. Her name really was appropriate. She was so small that her whole body was about the size of Tyson's head. Tiny blue, purple and sea green scales covered her body. Her little belly was swollen with the eggs that she'd be laying in the fall.

At first, he hadn't been too pleased with the addition of Rudenth to the property. Janie falling into Rudenth's lair had been terrifying and frankly, Rudenth's magic was the exact opposite of Tyson's. Where he was all fire and heat, she was water and cold. Tyson tended to keep his distance when they visited Rudenth's portion of the property, getting only close enough so as to make sure that none of the kids would fall in.

Not a problem this time because the only person with him was Giang Nunes, dryad and civil servant who was driving him slowly mad. Deidre was just as stuck on Giang as he was but Giang didn't seem to realize either of them were interested. And, given what xe'd said about assumptions other people had made, all he knew was that he didn't want to push xyr in the wrong way and lose completely any chance they had to have xyr around and get to know xyr better.

"Oh," Giang breathed, xyr hands clutched to xyr chest, her entire attention on the fairy dragon. "You're adorable!"

Where most dragons, either Oriental or Occidental, were human to house-sized lizard-types, Rudenth was the size of a kitten. Her scales glittered like gems and her tiny wings looked as delicate as iridescent soap bubbles stretched out over delicate translucent bones. But it was her magic that drew Giang most strongly. Most dragons felt of heat and fire. The Oriental types generally had a windy feel to them, especially as they slithered through the air.

Rudenth's magic felt like water, like rain dappling spring leaves. She drew Giang in much the way a spring drew the roots of a tree. Giang so wanted to pick her up and cuddle her, rub xyr face against Rudenth's little head and croon over her.

"Yes," Rudenth said with an assertive little nod. Her magic trilled the words into sounds they could all hear though, from the way Giang reacted, Tyson wondered if xe could have heard Rudenth even without the magic amplification. "Rudenth the Adorable. This is me. You are?"

"Goodness, I'm so sorry," Giang said as xyr cheeks blushed green with the faintest hints of red at the center. Xe held out one of xyr business cards, the laminated version that was green and leaf-shaped. "I'm Giang Nunes from the city government. My department is working on gathering the necessary items for the Harmony coming up in Belleview. I was hoping I could ask you for a bit of help."

Tyson tuned out as Giang launched into xyr lecture on what the Harmony was and how important it was to get pristine samples of the plants xe needed. He'd heard it six times now. The most recent had been when he took xem to meet Youneda and Felix on the theory that they might have ideas on where to look for the more elusive items.

Youneda and Felix had been in the area since just after the Opening, so they'd been a good guess. Not a successful one. Youneda had recommended going to check the sheep herding dragon clan, the Meo up in the Skagit. That'd failed, too.

Finding trilliums wasn't going to be easy, apparently. They used to bloom all through the Pacific Northwest, but the Opening had changed everything a hundred plus years ago. Tyson was halfway convinced that they'd gone extinct but Giang was certain that xe would find one eventually. It would be a miracle, really.

The Opening had torn apart the veil between the planes and jammed a thousand different worlds together into one patchwork. Over the last hundred or so years, after the Unification had stopped the fighting, all the species had worked to ease the patchwork bits together into a cohesive ecosystem but there was a lot of work left to be done. Their patch of woods was one of the larger undisturbed sections of Pacific Northwest temperate rainforest left.

Giang's smooth green bob swayed as xe gestured and explained to an entirely rapt Rudenth just what the Harmony would do for them all. Linking all the Elf enclaves so that they didn't disrupt the more material side of Belleview would be a good thing. Every week you heard about tourists getting lost in the Elves' pocket dimensions. Tyson didn't go that side of Lake Washington. He'd rather stay home with the kids and let Deidre deal with the Elves when pack business required it.

"Rudenth has not seen these flowers," Rudenth said thoughtfully, her little tail twitching like an excited cat's. "But Rudenth has not lived here very long. The water plants are easy. Rudenth can grow them for you without any issues. But Rudenth would like something in exchange."

That startled Tyson right out of his abstraction. Rudenth hadn't asked for anything other than a bridge over her creek since she moved in. Giang flapped a hand at Tyson without looking his way.

"What did you want?" Giang asked. Xe looked completely willing to give it to Rudenth if it would get xem the plants xe wanted.

"Visit?" Rudenth asked, teeny little hands clasped just over the swell of her egg-heavy belly. "Rudenth will be very busy tending the eggs once they are laid. It would be nice to have a visit from the pretty dryad-person Giang."

Giang blushed vividly green and clapped xyr hands over xyr cheeks. "Oh! Um. Yes? I'd be delighted to, actually. Dryads and fairy dragons have always got along well and you're the first one I ever met."

"Then Rudenth is the luckiest of dragons," Rudenth said. She put her little hands on Giang's knee, leaning closer in a blatantly seductive move that had Tyson staring at her. She even stretched her neck and fluttered her wings the way she would have for seducing another fairy dragon, despite the heavy swell of her belly weighing her down. "Rudenth would like very much to be friends with Giang."

"Friends," Giang said.

Xe beamed as xe very delicately rubbed right behind

Rudenth's ears. Tyson went back to leaning against the maple. Or tried to. He was a good bit too hot and even crossing his arms over his chest didn't make the heat go down.

Ten minutes later, Giang stood up and held xyr breath as Rudenth slid back into her creek, disappearing through the portal hidden under the little bridge they'd built. Tyson made himself breathe slowly, deeply, letting the heat and anger go. Giang wasn't his mate. Xe didn't show any signs of wanting to be mates with them. Or to be part of the pack, for that matter. He had no cause for being all up in Rudenth's face about her laying claim to Giang.

Even if Tyson really, really, really wished he and Deidre had gotten there first.

"You're tense," Giang said to him. Xe looked apologetic about it as xe headed back towards the house. "I'm sorry. The cold and water must have been disturbing for you."

"Oh, no, that's fine," Tyson said. His cheeks went hot with embarrassment this time, instead of magic mixed with rage. "I just hang back and there's no issue. No, it's just... well. I didn't quite like her asking you for things."

Giang blinked and stared up at him. Xyr eyes shifted color with xyr emotions. Green one moment, then brown as the duff below their feet, then as blue as the skies overhead. He still had no idea what the various colors meant though they did seem to be tied to Giang's emotions.

"It's silly of me," Tyson said. He tried for a reassuring tone instead of a possessive one. "You're perfectly free to agree to anything you want. And we love having you here so visiting as often as you like is fine. I'm just... well. Overreacting, honestly."

"Oh," Giang said. Xe patted Tyson's arm fondly. "Thank you for being so protective. Dryads do tend to be taken advantage of but I'm human enough that I'm quite capable of saying no. Just not to adorable tiny little fairy dragons with egg bumps on her belly."

Giang put xyr hands over xyr cheeks, so visibly delighted that Tyson found himself grinning at xem. How could anyone be so beautiful, so enticing, and have no idea whatsoever of it?

"She really is cute," Tyson agreed. "A little bit of a challenge for me but hey, that's just the conflicting magic. Mori adores her and goes out to visit on a regular basis."

"He's growing so much," Giang said as they entered the backyard. "I didn't think that I would see the difference in size in a matter of weeks."

Mori was there with Janie and August, each of whom held one of the twins, both of them in their human shape today rather than the more common pup form. Mimi was awake in Janie's arms but not for long. Her eyes were drooping. Cece had already fallen asleep in August's arms, draped over August like she was the best thing ever. Which, actually, she was. Fire-gifted baby cuddling in a fire spirit-dragon.

"Oh," Giang breathed.

Xyr eyes weren't pointed at the kids. Xe was staring at the pixie nest where a cloud of pixies had swarmed up and out, obviously on the hunt for prey as they had tiny spears in their hands and nets. Hunting for sparrows, then. When they went after mice or rats, or even insects, pixies didn't bother with spears or nets. They just bit. Sparrows were too fast for that, though, so they needed to augment their mouths that were already full of razor-sharp teeth.

"Scared?" Tyson asked protectively.

"Not at all," Giang murmured. Xe stood and watched as the pixies flew up into the sky, puffs of white, pink and blue hair looking like an ever-shifting cloud as sunrise. "I've never seen such a strong flock before. They're quite healthy. Bigger than normal."

Tyson snorted. "That's what happens when you give them what they need to survive and respect their right to live, love and have children. Deidre just about went feral when she realized that all the laws keeping pixies from making new nests was keeping them from breeding."

"I remember that council meeting," Giang said with a huge grin. "She was so fierce. And right. The pixies have as much of a right to live as anyone else. The mayor is working on setting up approved locations for them but it's a bit of a conflict with the pigeons. They tend to like the same territories and don't get along at all. Though that does make sense. Pixies are predators and pigeons know it."

Tyson stared. Honestly stared. Which had the result of making Giang blink and then start laughing. It was a gorgeous laugh, full of snorts and wheezes, snickers that wrinkled xyr nose. He wouldn't have thought that his heart could squeeze any more than it already did around Giang but here he was, a half-step away from clutching his chest.

"Everyone forgets the pigeons," Giang finally said, grinning at him. "They're pets, you know. Humans bred them to be docile, to be useful, for generations. Just like dogs and sheep and horses. But they forgot about it with the pigeons. It's sad. Pigeons just want to be loved. So of course we make sure they have nice safe roosts and plenty of clean food and water. They don't wander or cause trouble when their roosts are safe."

"I... honestly had no idea," Tyson said. "I've never seen a pigeon. They don't come out here."

Giang nodded. "No, they wouldn't. Too many predators and pixies in this area. That's why the mayor is working so hard to find good places for the pixies. Their territories can't overlap with the pigeons'. Or each other's. I don't think we need pixie battles in the sky."

"Definitely not," Tyson agreed.

He'd seen a few of those. Most everyone in the suburb had. Before they'd let the pixie cloud settled under their deck, three local bands of pixies had done battle repeatedly in the sky over their heads to claim territory. It was part of why Deidre had offered to let the pixies stay.

"Would you, ah, like to come in for some tea?" Tyson offered nervously. He just couldn't keep the nerves out of his voice, or the shake out of his hands.

"I'd love to," Giang said with xyr brightest grin. "As beautiful as Rudenth is, she's very cold. Clearly from one of the colder regions. I mean, I thought she was just the sweetest thing I've ever seen but now I'm chilled right through."

Xyr lips were green. So were xyr fingertips which were normally pink-toned. Tyson bustled xem right into the house and into the kitchen which, thankfully, was empty right now. It wouldn't last. There wasn't much time before Deidre got home with the day's groceries. Enough, hopefully, for him to brew Giang some tea and maybe, possibly, if he was really lucky, find a way to show Giang that he and Deidre were interested in xem without scaring xem away. From what he'd already seen, xe did tend to be skittish about anything relationship oriented though Tyson had no idea why. Xe were sweet and kind and the kids adored xem, just like Tyson and Rudenth did. He had no idea how anyone wouldn't want to have Giang around.

Giang took xyr mug of tea and cradled it close to xyr chest. "Oh, goodness, that's wonderful. I'm from alpine dryad stock, aspens and the like, but I do love my warmth."

"I could... warm you up?" Tyson offered, barely able to contain himself from flooding the kitchen with heat just at the thought of wrapping his magic around Giang.

"Could you?" Giang asked only to shake xyr head and smile. "Silly of me. Of course you could. Yes, please. I'm quite cold and I shouldn't drive like this. Slows the reactions down terribly."

"Stay right there," Tyson said.

He didn't have permission to touch xyr, so he carefully let his magic spread through the room. Heat, no fire attached, flowed outwards from his body. Tyson used his hands to sculpt the heat so that it swirled around Giang. Who sighed and smiled as xe closed xyr eyes and sipped the tea like it was the best thing ever.

Delicate green strands of hair drifted across Giang's cheek, shifting under the flow of heated air. Xe lifted xyr chin and Tyson sent more warmth down xyr neck, pooling in the pocket between Giang's chest and arms. Xe leaned forward, mouth open slightly and eyes shimmering with a reddish tint that he'd never seen before. They gleamed, too, brighter than he thought was normal. As if Giang's magic was reacting to Tyson's.

"We're home!" Deidre called from the back door.

Giang jerked and stood, eyes wide with sudden panic. Xe set down the mug of tea and grabbed xyr bag. "I should go. Thank you for escorting me, Tyson."

"No, you... don't have to go," Tyson sighed as Giang ran out of the kitchen and out the back door.

He heard Deidre exclaim something but when he looked around the corner Giang was long gone.

Deidre raised an eyebrow and Tyson groaned as he let her pull him into her arms. She rubbed his back and kissed his forehead.

"Didn't get a chance to tell xem you're interested?" Deidre asked.

"I don't know," Tyson groaned. "I thought we might have

had a connection there but then xe spooked when you came in. I just. I don't know."

Deidre chuckled. "I'll talk to xem next time xe visits. Come on. Help me bring the groceries in."

Tyson nodded and followed her outside. Damn it all.

Ten Days of Harmony is now available at all major retailers in ebook and TPB format.

OTHER BOOKS BY MEYARI
MCFARLAND:

Day Hunt on the Final Oblivion

Day of Joy

Immortal Sky

A New Path

Following the Trail

Crafting Home

Finding a Way

Go Between

Like Arrows of Fate

Out of Disaster

The Shores of Twilight Bay

Coming Together

Following the Beacon

The Solace of Her Clan

You can find these and many other books at www.MDR-Publishing.com. We are a small independent publisher focusing on LGBT content. Please sign up for our mailing list to get regular updates on the latest preorders and new releases and a free ebook!

AFTERWORD

My favorite "robe" is a fleece blanket that has armholes cut in it and a matching fleece wrap. They're the softest things I've every touched, just lovely to snuggle up in. My "robe" is what inspired this particular story.

Snuggling up warm in a fleecy bit of joy while slowly and calmly making sure that everything is right in the world is a deeply lovely experience. Having a warm bed and someone you love to come back to is even better.

I hope you have warmth, happiness and family in your lives that give you just as much joy.

If you want more stories like this one, please go sign up for my newsletter on www.MDR-Publishing.com. You'll get updates on whatever I've got coming up, special deals and you can get a free ebook or collection of my short stories. Or you can sign up at my Patreon and get access to my art, writing and whatever's going on creatively in my life.

Thank you for reading!

Meyari McFarland

March, 2024
www.MDR-Publishing.com

AUTHOR BIO

Meyari McFarland has been telling stories since she was a small child. Her stories range from adventures appropriate to children to erotica but they always feature strong characters who do what they think is right no matter what gets in their way.

Meyari has been married for twenty years and has no children or pets. She lives in the Puget Sound, WA and enjoys the fog, rain and cool weather that are typical here. When vacation times come, she and her husband usually go somewhere warm like Hawaii or they go on their own adventures to Japan and other far away countries.

Her life has included jobs ranging from cleaning motel rooms, food service, receptionist, building and editing digital maps, auditing and document control.

MORE FROM MEYARI MCFARLAND

Website:

. . .

www.MDR-Publishing.com

SOCIAL MEDIA:

Patreon - https://www.patreon.com/meyarimcfarland
Mastodon – https://wandering.shop/@MeyariMcFarland
Pillowfort - https://www.pillowfort.social/Meyari
Facebook - https://www.facebook.com/meyari.mcfarland.5
Pinterest - https://www.pinterest.com/meyarim/

*If you enjoyed this story, **please leave a comment on your favorite site. Also, please sign up for the newsletter so that you can hear about the latest preorders and new releases.***

www.ingramcontent.com/pod-product-compliance
Lightning Source LLC
LaVergne TN
LVHW042004060526
838200LV00041B/1867